Penny the DINOSAUR

Who forgot her Birthday

Written and Illustrated by

Michael Salmon

Murray David

How to pronounce the dinosaur and prehistoric animal names in this book

Iguanodon (Toothed lizard)
IG-WA-NO-DON

Dimetrodon (Two sized teeth)
DI-MET-RO-DON

Triceratops (Three horned face)
TRY-SER-A-TOPS

Apatosaurus (Deceptive lizard - Two sized teeth)
A-PAT-UH-SAW-RUS

Stegosaurus (Roofed lizard)
STEG-UH-SAW-RUS

Pterodactyl (Winged fingers)
TAIR-UH-DAK-TILL

Published by
Murray David Publishing
35 Borgnis Street, Davidson, New South Wales, 2085, Australia
Postal Address: P.O. Box 140, Belrose West, New South Wales, 2085, Australia
Phone: 61 2 9451 3895 Fax: 61 2 9451 3663
www.m2d.com.au
email: mail@m2d.com.au

This large format edition first published 2008
Publishing Director: Marion Child
Marketing Director: David Jenkins
Executive Director: David Forsythe
Designed by Emma Sutton
Digital photography by the late James Young
Copyright © Monster Promotions Pty Ltd, 2008
Copyright © in layout M2D Publishing Pty Ltd, 2008
ISBN: 978-1-876411-54-1

Printed in Indonesia

Iguanodon

The iguanodon tooth that was found in 1822 started all the interest and research into dinosaurs that there is today (no one really knew much about dinosaurs until then).

When the iguanodon stood up it was about as high as a big semi-trailer and was as heavy as an elephant. It lived in herds in the warm, swampy countryside eating the trees and shrubs. The iguanodon had a spikey thumb that might have been used to protect itself and was certainly useful in tearing down branches of tasty leaves. It could have run well on its hind legs or walked on all fours.

One morning, as **PENNY** the iguanodon woke up, she had the strange feeling that for some reason today was a very special day.

'Perhaps it's because the sun is shining so brightly?' she thought, as she ate some leaves for breakfast.

'I wonder what my friends are doing today?'
said Penny, as she wandered off towards the
volcano where the dimetrodons lived.

'I'm sorry, Penny, you can't come any further!' said one of the older dimetrodons. 'We are making something special and no one is allowed to see it.'

Before Penny could find out what the dimetrodons were making, she smelled something nice in the air. 'It must be the triceratops cooking food in the hot lava pools. I'll go and see them,' she said.

'I'm sorry, Penny,' said one of the triceratops.
'We can't stop to talk to you now. We're much
too busy. Please come back later!'

'This is very strange,' thought Penny. 'The triceratops have never been too busy before. I'll visit the apatosaurs instead. They're never too busy.'

But Penny was wrong. The apatosaurs were wrapping things up in large painted leaves. When they saw Penny, they hid what they were wrapping. Penny felt that the apatosaurs didn't want her around, so she walked on.

Penny began to feel very sad. Even the Stegosaur Band stopped their singing and playing, then walked away when they saw Penny.

'Perhaps today isn't special after all!'
thought Penny, as she walked back to the
forest. She pushed slowly through the tree
ferns.

"HAPPY BIRTHDAY" to you!

Suddenly – **SURPRISE, SURPRISE, HAPPY BIRTHDAY!** sang all the dinosaurs! It was a surprise birthday party for Penny and Penny had completely forgotten that it was her birthday! She was so happy that she almost cried. There were painted ribbons and signs on the trees.

'We're sorry we couldn't talk to you when you came to see us,' said the dimetrodons. 'But we would have spoiled the surprise.'

'Here are your presents,' said the apatosaurs.
'We wrapped them in painted leaves for you.'

There was a bouncy pillow made from springy swamp roots. There was a pretty necklace made of painted stones and two statues carved out of wood.

The triceratops carried in a very large
birthday cake, which had a candle placed
carefully in the centre of it.

The Stegosaur Band began to sing...
'Happy Birthday, dear Penny,
Happy Birthday to you.
Happy Birthday, dear Penny,
Happy Birthday to you.'
Penny blew out the candle with one blow
and each dinosaur had a slice of cake. It
was delicious!

After the cake was eaten, the dinosaurs played party games.

Penny liked to play 'Pin the tail on the pterodactyl'. The pterodactyl didn't mind because the tail was only a vine with some sticky glue on it.

The dinosaurs laughed when the tail got
stuck on the nose of an apatosaurus!

Penny's very special day had come to an end, but Penny knew that this was one birthday she would never forget!

Dinosaurs

The dinosaurs were land animals that ruled the world for over 140 million years. The last dinosaurs died out about 60 million years before people first appeared.

The name dinosaur means 'terrible lizard'. They were a special group of prehistoric reptiles, and their closest living relative is the crocodile.

Dinosaurs grew far larger than any land animal alive today. Just one of the largest dinosaurs would have weighed more than 1 500 people!

However, there were some dinosaurs that grew no bigger than a chicken. They came in many shapes and sizes; some plodded on all fours, some walked and ran on their hind legs like ostriches.

There were both fierce meat-eating dinosaurs and ones that ate plants. Some lived on hills, others roamed low plains and dry areas. Most preferred the lush forests that covered large areas of the Earth.

It wasn't until the last century that people realised dinosaurs had actually existed. Since then, thousands of skeletons have been collected all over the world.